A WRITERS MATTER INITIATIVE

Missing Pop

A story about Loving and Remembering Pop

Written by
Bob Vogel and Leo Rosner
Illustrated by Luna Saieh

Publisher's Name: Bob Vogel and Leo Rosner

Paperback ISBN: 978-1-971601 08 3

About This Book

The central character in this story is an inquisitive and caring ten-year-old boy who is learning to find his own way through the death of his grandfather, Pop. Through vivid memories and deeply personal experiences, he discovers how to celebrate Pop's life in a way that feels meaningful to him—through storytelling. Missing Pop is a story about love, loss, and remembrance. It emphasizes the importance of keeping memories alive and helps children understand that grieving can also include celebrating the life of someone they loved. The book encourages children to express their thoughts, feelings, and emotions as they navigate a difficult time and begin to heal.

Dedication Page

To My Pop, who taught me so much and remains in my heart each day as I grow older. And, to all the children celebrating the memories of their grandparents.

Special Shout-Out to Leo's parents, Lauren and Jake, whose support and love encouraged Leo to bring Leo's memories of his Pop to paper.

Interactive Feature

This book encourages readers to reflect on and respond to the personal experiences of the main character. Each reader brings their own story, and the book includes an interactive feature called **"Time to Wonder or Doodle,"** inviting children to write, draw, imagine possible solutions, share observations, and connect the story to their own experiences. Most importantly, the blue bubble creates a space where each reader's voice can be heard—an empowering way for children to explore their own thoughts, feelings, and personal challenges.

Time to Wonder or DOODLE

Missing Pop – A story about Loving and Remembering Pop

The chair that Pop always sat in is still there.
It looks so different now that it is empty.
It doesn't feel the same without him there.

I can still picture him sleeping on the blue lounge chair.
He seems so alive and full of life to me.
I can almost hear him breathing; he seems so peaceful.
I like getting close to the lounge chair, sometimes just touching it gently.

When I go past the chair, I say, "Hi Pop" – it makes me feel happy.
Sometimes, I sit in the chair – it is comforting to me and feels so special.

I stand very still, quietly.
If I sit there long enough, I will hear him sneeze –
so loud, sometimes it would scare me.

The sound of the TV stayed well after he fell asleep.
He loved to listen to the news, especially on Sunday morning.

I look around the room, and everything feels so different now.
The warm feeling I remembered that Pop brought to the room is not there anymore.
I wonder where Pop went.
I wonder what happened to his body.
I wonder if Pop can see me, hear me.
It makes me sad in so many ways.
I have so many questions.

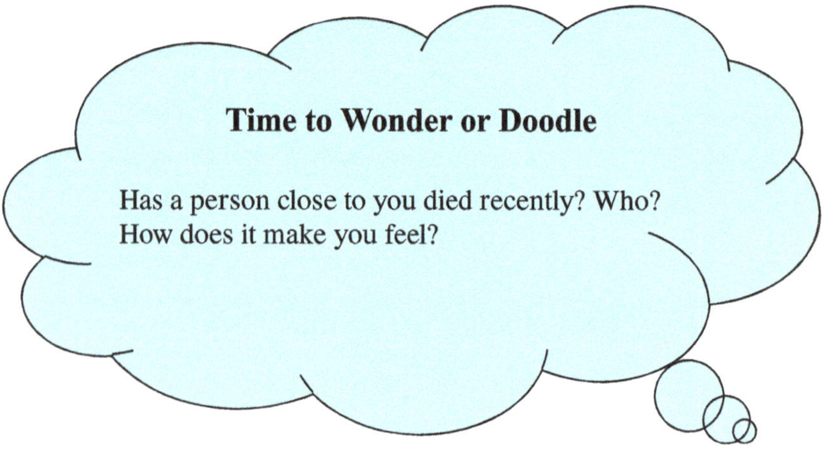

At dinner, we talk about Pop.

We have so many fun memories.
Mom remembers dancing and laughing with Pop.
Dad remembers cooking with Pop and
helping him with his computer.
My little brother remembers watching golf and March Madness with Pop.
Pop loved being with the family.
We loved being with him.

I guess I will never see Pop again.
I am missing Pop.
I loved Pop.

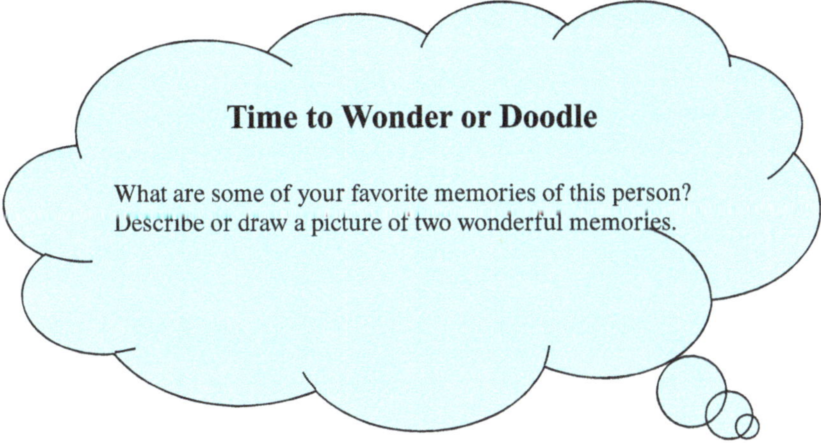

There are so many pictures of Pop and our family
all over the house.
Grammy made picture books, and you can find
them everywhere.
Sometimes I pick them up and turn the pages slowly,
looking for my favorite pictures and staring at them...
I like to stare at them and think of Pop
I like to touch the pictures with my fingers. It makes
me feel closer to Pop.

Sometimes during the day, I suddenly feel sad. I really miss Pop.
My Mom told me that my younger brother gets sad too, especially when he is in school.
His mind wanders—just like mine.
I think it is a good thing, because I like thinking about Pop.
I guess that is OK.

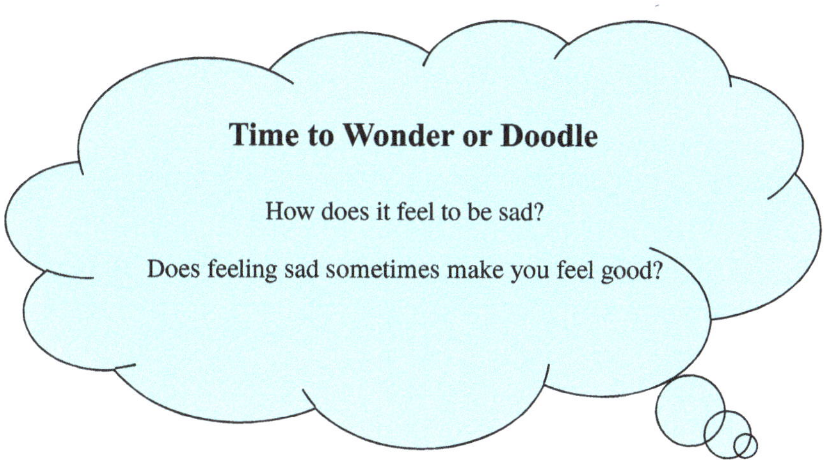

Pop loved to paint.

I heard he was an art teacher when he was younger.
Pop's paintings are all over our house.
I didn't look at them much before he died, but now I do.
When I go past one of the pictures, I can feel Pop—it makes me smile.

My favorite picture Pop drew is one on the beach with a big flag.
I have it hanging in my room.
There is an old guy standing in the water.
It reminds me of Pop.
Pop loved to watch my cousins and me swim in the ocean. He was always there for us—he made us feel safe.

When Pop died, I drew a picture of the beach painting just like his picture that hangs in my bedroom.
I put the picture in his casket so he would remember me.
I wrote a note to Pop telling him, "I will never forget you Pop, I love you".
I bet he smiled when he saw it.

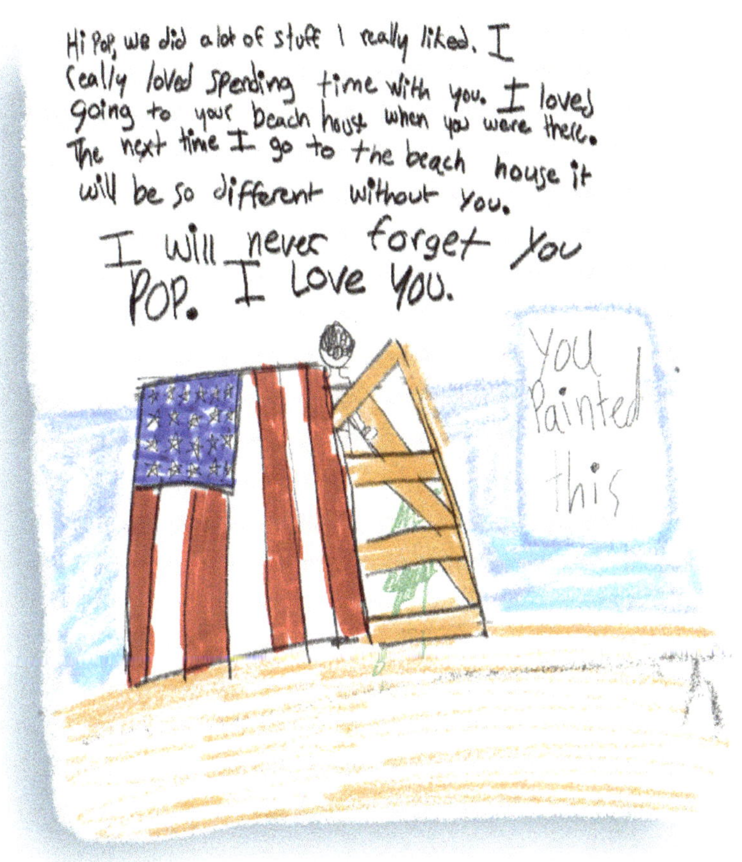
Hi Pop, we did alot of stuff I really liked. I
really loved spending time with you. I loved
going to your beach house when you were there.
The next time I go to the beach house it
will be so different without you.
I will never forget you
Pop. I love you.
You
Painted
this

Time to Wonder or Doodle

Describe a fun memory you shared with this person that made you feel happy.

Sometimes Pop let me help him paint.

Pop would play his favorite music while painting, and
he played it so loud. He loved his music.
He used so many bright colors and never worried if I made a mess.
He let me hold his brush and put it into the paint.
I can still feel his warm hand holding mine.
If I spilled the paint on the floor, – he never yelled at me.
He was always smiling when he painted.
I am going to miss painting with him—maybe I will become a painter just like him.

Pop used to take me on his boat.

It was an adventure with the whole family.
Sometimes he let me sit on his lap and steer across the water.
Other times, we sat together at the back of the boat while my dad drove.
I can see Pop and even feel him—it feels so good.

When I think about it, I can still feel the wind on my face,
Pop's warm arms around me.
It makes me feel happy inside.
Pop would also take me on his jet ski.

We were going so fast that I had tears coming from my eyes.
I held on tight because the waves made us bounce.
My hair was flying everywhere,
and water splashed on my face—it was so fun.

I felt brave.
I felt safe.
I felt so loved.

Pop made a special toasted cheese sandwich just for me.
The cheese was so gooey and sometimes got all over my face.
I miss those sandwiches—nobody in the world can make them the way he did.

I will never get to taste that again since Pop is not here anymore.

Pop made a toasted bagel sandwich for himself.
He put tomatoes, cream cheese, and other stuff he liked on it.
I can still smell those sandwiches - and remember the taste so well.
I can still hear the "crunch sound" Pop made when he was eating the sandwich.
I am going to learn how to make those sandwiches just like Pop.
It will make him so happy and will help me always remember Pop.

Pop and I would Facetime often and play on the computer together.
He made silly faces and funny sounds that made me laugh.
His silliest sound was "Yayayayayayayaya!"
I miss that sound so much.

Pop loved to be with me, my brother, and my two cousins.
He taught us how to be kind and help others that didn't have all the things we had.
Every 4th of July, we would set up a stand outside our house. We made signs and sold lemonade and cookies. With all the money we made, Pop helped us decide which
charities to give the money to.
He taught us so many things—that is why I love him so much.

When Pop was sick, his face got puffy and turned red like tomatoes.

He pushed his cheeks in and out to make me laugh.
I think he liked making me laugh and seeing me happy.
When I think of Pop now, I feel happy first.
Then I feel sad because he isn't here anymore.
It feels confusing for me, but my memories are so fun.
I guess it is Ok to feel both.

Pop laughed a lot and made me feel everything was OK.
When he got sick, he didn't laugh a lot.
But he did smile a lot—especially with me.
Sometimes I wonder if he thinks of me now.
I don't know where he is.
I hope he is still smiling.

Time to Wonder or Doodle

Describe or draw a picture of the two of you together when you were having fun.

Pop isn't around anymore to go boating with me.

He isn't here to make bagel sandwiches or for me to watch him sleeping with the TV on. I will never hear his giant sneeze again.

But his paintings are still here with so many colors.
My memories are still here.
When I close my eyes,
I can still feel the wind on my face.
I can still hear his silly sounds.
I can still feel his warm hands.

I miss Pop.
I remember Pop.
I love Pop.

I know Pop is still looking after me.
When I was sick the other night, I asked Pop to make me feel better.
when I went to sleep.
The next morning, I woke up and I felt so much better.
My Pop is always there for me—always.
My loving feeling for Pop will never go away.

Pop used to tell me I was strong.

I can still hear him looking at me and saying, 'You are so strong.'
When I remember him,
I feel strong again.

I love Pop
for helping me feel strong.

"Pop isn't here anymore. But loving Pop is still here."
I will never stop "Missing Pop".

Here's a game to play. Here is what I wrote about Pop. You might want to try this yourself – It sure helped me remember Pop.

My Memory Arcade – Creating memories

What food reminds you of your grandparent? Bage toasted ham, and tomatoes.

Your turn________________________________

What were your favorite sounds? Waves banging ag boat, Pop sneezing, and Pop telling me I was strong

Your turn________________________________

How did your grandparent make you feel when you around them? Did they make you feel happy, safe, l

Your turn________________________________

If you had a chance to talk to your grandparent aga now, what would you say? I miss you so much, you me laugh all the time, you were so much fun.

Your turn________________________________

Parent, Teacher, and Caregiver Guide

Notes From the Author

You are probably reading this book because you are helping a child cope with the loss of someone they love. That person may be a grandparent, parent, sibling, relative, or friend. One of the most important things for children — and for adults as well — is to understand that they are not alone. Creating a safe space to talk about loss and building a caring support community can make a meaningful difference.

When a special person in a child's life dies, the child may experience many different thoughts, feelings, and emotions. They might feel sad, angry, confused, worried, disappointed, or lonely. At times, they may even feel happy when they remember fun or loving moments they shared. These feelings can change from day to day or even from hour to hour. These emotional ups and downs are a normal part of the grieving process.

It is important to remember that love does not disappear when someone dies. Children often carry many memories inside them. Some memories are shared right away, while others take time to surface. Adults can help children cope by gently encouraging them to talk about these memories. Remembering helps children stay connected to the people they miss.

Children's memories may come in many forms. They may recall shared experiences, favorite jokes, special foods, hugs, holding hands, or silly sounds. Smells, pictures, music, and familiar places can also bring memories and feelings back in powerful ways.

Talking about the person who died can be very comforting. Encouraging a child to draw pictures, write in a journal, or tell stories can help them express what they are feeling. Adults can also share their own memories, creating an environment where the child feels supported, understood, and not alone.

It is important for children to know that everyone experiences grief differently. There is no right or wrong way to miss someone. Each child's feelings and reactions are unique.

The story in this book shares one child's experience of coping with the loss of his grandfather, Pop. Throughout the story, "Wonder Questions" invite children to reflect on their own memories and feelings. You may wish to encourage children to write or draw their responses. This interactive approach helps give children a voice and may even inspire them to create their own stories of love and remembrance.

By listening with patience, sharing memories, and allowing space for feelings, we help children discover that love can continue to guide and strengthen them throughout their lives.

I created this parent guide to help you navigate the challenging process of supporting your child through grief after the loss of a loved one. I hope you find it beneficial.
Please note that this guide includes many of my own ideas and insights from my experiences as a teacher and parent, along with information collected, summarized, and edited from ChatGPT, Gemini, and Copilot.

Bob

Parent, Teacher, and Caregiver Guide

Helping Children Cope with Loss and Celebrating the Life of a Loved One.

This guide is designed to support children as they learn to adapt to the loss of someone they love. It emphasizes the importance of keeping memories alive while allowing children to express their thoughts, feelings, and emotions in a safe and supportive environment.

When a child loses a loved one, they may experience feelings they have never felt before. These emotions can be complex, confusing, intense, painful, and sometimes unexpected. Children between the ages of **8 and 12** are beginning to understand that death is permanent, yet they may still struggle to fully process what it means or find the words to express how they feel. As adults, we play an important role in helping them navigate this difficult experience.

This guide offers ideas and strategies to help create a safe space where children can share memories, express emotions, and begin to heal. *A key point is that children should never go through grieving alone – they need to have the comfort and understanding of others.*

This guide can be used at home, in classrooms, or in counseling settings.

Key Points

Understanding How Children Grieve

- Children grieve differently from adults. They could seem perfectly fine one moment and then become very sad the next.
- The child may move **in and out of sadness quickly**, appearing

fine one moment and upset the next.

- Here are some common reactions by children when grieving:

  1. Asking many questions about death
  2. Worrying about where the person is now
  3. Difficulty concentrating in school
  4. Sudden sadness or tears
  5. Irritability or withdrawal
  6. Wanting to talk about memories often
  7. Laughing or playing normally (this is healthy)

Listening to Children's Feelings

Children often want to talk about their feelings, even if it is not immediately obvious. When a child chooses to share, it is important for adults to be ready to listen with patience and care.

Here are some helpful ways to support them:

1. Give your full attention when a child wants to talk.
2. Stay calm, even when questions feel difficult.
3. Avoid judging, correcting, or dismissing their feelings
4. Try to see the situation from the child's perspective and stay away from adult responses.
5. Don't expect responses instantaneously—kids need "think time" to process information.
6. Resist the urge to "fix" the feeling — focus on listening

Suggested prompts when listening to a child:

- "That sounds really hard for you."

- "Can you tell me more about what you're feeling—maybe using one or two words."
- "What do you miss the most about them?"
- "I'm really glad you shared that with me."
- "Thank you for trusting me with your feelings.".

How to Help Children talk about Sadness:

Some children talk easily about grief. Others need gentle encouragement and time.

You can help by:

Sharing your own memories of someone you have lost.
Looking at family photos together
Holding or remembering familiar objects that belonged to the loved one
Reading *Loving Pop* and pausing to reflect
Asking open-ended questions that have no right or wrong answer

Conversation starters that are comfortable:

- "What is one fun memory you have?"
- "Are there certain times of day when you miss them the most?"
- "If you could talk to them right now, what would you say?"
- "What reminds you of them — a place, a smell, a food, a sound?"
- "What do you think they would want you to remember?"

Interactive memory strategies to help continue a connection

Remembering helps children feel less alone and reassures them that love continues even after someone dies. Try some of these memory games:

- Creating a memory box — see activity at the end of the story in the book
- Drawing pictures of favorite moments — can be stick figures or drawings. Use crayons or color pencils. Colors allow for expression of feelings.
- Writing a brief poem, song or letter to the person who died
- Cooking or preparing a favorite shared food. For example, the bagel sandwich in the book.
- Visiting meaningful places or sharing familiar routines—TV show they shared.
- Remembering how holidays, birthdays, or traditions were celebrated.

When Children Feel Confused or Afraid

Children may worry about:

- Who might die next
- Whether they caused the death
- What happens to the body
- Whether the person can still see or hear them

Adults can offer simple reassurance:

- "Nothing you did caused this."
- "Most people live for a very long time."
- "You are safe and cared for."

Open conversations help children feel secure.

Helping Children Find Strength Within

Over time, many children discover that memories can become a **source of comfort and strength.**

You can gently reinforce this by saying:

- "Their love is part of you."
- "What did they teach you that you still carry?"
- "How can we honor them together?"

These conversations support healing, resilience, and emotional growth.

Key Family Takeaways

- Grief is not something children simply "get over." They need time, support, and understanding.
- Listening, remembering, and sharing stories helps children feel connected and safe.
- Completing the "Wonder Questions" in *Loving Pop* can help children express their thoughts.
- Missing someone reflects the depth of love they shared.
- Love can remain a lifelong source of comfort and strength.

Activities

Memory Box Ideas – These are fun activities allowing children to use some of their skill sets to express themselves.

Children may include:

- Photos or drawings
- A favorite object or small keepsake
- A note, poem, or letter
- Something that reminds them of the person

Memory Reflection Prompts

- A sound I remember: __________
- A smell or taste I remember: __________
- A place we went together: __________

Encourage children to create a short phrase or saying that helps them feel comforted, such as:

- "My memories make me strong."
- "Love stays with me."
- "It's okay to talk about my feelings."

Remember, some days children may feel very sad.
Other days may bring laughter, comfort, and warm memories.
Both are part of learning to live with loss.
Their voices need to be heard.
Just as important, they need opportunities to celebrate the life of someone they loved and lost.

About the authors:

Bob Vogel, Ed.D., holds a doctorate in Educational Psychology and Organizational Development from Temple University. After 43 years of teaching in the Department of Education at La Salle University, Bob retired and now serves as Professor Emeritus of Education.
In 2005, he became the Founding Director of Writers Matter, a nonprofit organization that helps young students develop writing skills through personal journaling. Writers Matter works with approximately 4,500 children in Philadelphia, as well as high school students in Israel. Writers Matter Israel brings Israeli and Palestinian students together to find commonalities and mutual understanding through writing.

Bob's most recent books include *Honest*, *Becoming Me*, *Wondering: Feelings, Emotions, and Building Resilience*, *Standing Tall, Standing Strong*, *Sam's Story: A Journey of Self-Discovery*, *The Write Path: Israeli and Palestinian Youth Finding Commonalities and Mutual Understanding Through Writing*, and *The Write Path II:*

Hope — Israeli and Palestinian Youth Finding Hope and Empathy Through Writing.

Bob lives in Philadelphia with his wife, Marlyn. He has two sons and three granddaughters. He enjoys writing, biking, conversations with his granddaughters, traveling with his wife, and helping young people find their voices through writing.

Leo Rosner is entering 4th grade at Kresson Elementary School. Leo enjoys playing baseball, video games, guitar, Legos, magic, and biking around the neighborhood. He spends his time hanging out with his friends and quality time with his family. Leo is inquisitive, thoughtful, hard-working, and fun to be around.

About the Illustrator

Luna Saieh is a 12th-grade student working towards a profession in animation and illustration. She has had a passion for visual storytelling for as long as she can remember. Luna strives to improve her capabilities in any way she can and hopes to one day be able to create stories of her own.

Books Published by Bob Vogel

Honest: Becoming Me (co-authored with Andre Saunders)
Wondering: *Feelings, Emotions and Building Resilience*
Standing Tall Standing Strong
Sam's Story: *A Journey of Self-Discovery*
The Write Path II: Hope – Israeli and Palestinian Youth Finding Hope and Empathy Through Writing - (co-authored with Steven Aiello)
The Write Path – *Israeli and Palestinian Youth Finding Commonalities and Mutual Understanding Through Writing.* (co-authored with Steven Aiello)

Empowering Young Writers: *The "Writers Matter" Approach*
Voices of Teens: *Writers Matter*

Writers Matter Website – Use QR Code or www.writersmatter.org